'WE D
AN O

FRANZ KAFKA
Born 1883, Prague, Austria-Hungary
Died 1924, Kierling, Austria

Forschungen eines Hundes was written in 1922, and published
posthumously in *Beim Bau der Chinesischen Mauer* in 1931.
The first English translation, by Willa and Edwin Muir,
was published in 1933.

KAFKA IN PENGUIN MODERN CLASSICS
Amerika
The Burrow
The Castle
The Great Wall of China
Metamorphosis and Other Stories
The Trial

FRANZ KAFKA

Investigations of a Dog

Translated by Michael Hofmann

PENGUIN BOOKS

PENGUIN CLASSICS

UK | USA | Canada | Ireland | Australia
India | New Zealand | South Africa

Penguin Books is part of the Penguin Random House group
of companies whose addresses can be found at
global.penguinrandomhouse.com.

Penguin
Random House
UK

This edition first published 2018

001

Set in 11.2/13.75 pt Dante MT Std
Typeset by Jouve (UK), Milton Keynes
Printed in Great Britain by Clays Ltd, St Ives plc

ISBN: 978–0–241–33930–5

www.greenpenguin.co.uk

How my life has changed, and in other ways, hardly at all! When I remember the times when I was still living in the midst of dogs, taking part in everything that concerned them – a dog among dogs – I do find on closer examination that there was always something not quite right about the picture, a little breach or rupture; a mild unease would befall me at the heart of the most respected tribal occasions, yes, sometimes even in intimate settings; no, not just sometimes, but very often, the sight of a dear fellow dog, his mere aspect, somehow seen afresh, could make me embarrassed, shocked, alarmed – yes, even desperate. I tried to calm myself, friends I discussed it with helped me, quieter times came along, times that were not free of such surprises either, only they were accepted in a spirit of greater equanimity, were more casually absorbed into the tissue of life; perhaps they made me sad and tired, but they allowed me to continue to exist as a perhaps somewhat aloof, reserved, frightened, calculating, but all in all regulation dog. How – without these pauses for refreshment – could I ever have reached my proud age; how could I have forced my way through to the calm with which I observe the terrors of my youth and bear the terrors of my seniority; how could I ever have learned to draw the correct conclusions from my admittedly unhappy or, putting it more cautiously, not so terribly happy constitution and live almost entirely by their light? Withdrawn, solitary, entirely taken up with my small, hopeless but – to me – indispensable inquiries, that's how I live, but in so doing I never lost sight of my people from a distance, often news of them reached me, and from time to time I let them hear of my doings. I am treated with respect – they don't understand my way of living, but they don't hold it against me and even young dogs I see running by in the distance from time to time, a new generation, whose infancy I can barely recall, do not deny me a respectful greeting.

It would be wrong to suppose that, for all my – all too apparent – eccentricities, I have completely lost touch with the species. If I think about it, and I have the time and inclination and capacity to do so, we dogs are an odd lot. Apart from ourselves, there are many other creatures round about – poor, inadequate, mute beings, restricted to the odd squawk at best – we have studied them, given them names, tried to help them along, to ennoble them, and so on and so forth, but to me, so long as they don't bother me, they are a matter of indifference. I get them mixed up or ignore them, but one thing remains too striking for me ever to forget it, and that is how little, compared to us dogs, they consort, how they pass by one another like strangers, how they have neither high nor low interests in common, how on the contrary any interests they have seem to drive them further apart than they already are. Whereas we dogs! One may surely say that we live in a pack, all of us, however different we may be in terms of the innumerable and profound distinctions that have arisen between us over the ages. All one pack! We are impelled to be together, and nothing can prevent us from satisfying that urge; all our laws and institutions, the few I still know, and the numberless ones I have forgotten, they all go back to the greatest happiness that exists for us, our warm companionableness. And now the obverse. No creature to the best of my knowledge lives in such a dispersed way as we dogs, none has so many, so impossibly many differences of kind, of breed, of occupation. We, who want to be together – and repeatedly we are able to, at moments of exaltation – we of all creatures live remote from one another, in curious callings, which are often hard for the dog next door to understand, clinging to regulations that are not of our making – yes, that seem, if anything, to be directed against us. These are such difficult matters, matters one would prefer not to interfere with – I understand such a point of view, understand it better than my own – and yet I have allowed them to govern my life. Why do I not do as others do, live in harmony with my people, and accept in silence what disturbs the harmony, ignore it like a small error in a large reckoning, and keep my eye on the thing that links us happily together, not that which repeatedly and irresistibly rips us out of our community . . .

I remember an incident from my youth. I was in one of those inexplicable states of blissful excitement that we probably all experience as children – I was still a very young dog, liking everything, attached to everything. I believed that great things were happening around me, whose focus I was, to which I needed to lend my voice, things that would be condemned to lie languishing on the ground if I didn't run on their behalf, swing my body around for them – childish fantasies that recede over the years, but at that time they were very strong, I was wholly in thrall to them – and then something quite extraordinary happened, which seemed to confirm these wild expectations of mine. Intrinsically it was nothing extraordinary, and later on I saw such things, and others, still stranger, quite regularly, but at the time it struck me with a primal, powerful, indelible impression that set the tone for much that followed. I encountered a small group of dogs, or rather I didn't encounter them, they approached me. I had then been running around for a long time in the dark, with a presentiment of great things, a presentiment that was a little misleading admittedly, because it was always with me. I had long been running through the darkness, this way and that, guided by nothing but a vague yearning, then suddenly I stopped with the sense that I was in the right place, I looked up, and it was a full dazzling day, with just a little heat-haze. I greeted the morning with confused sounds, then – just as if I had summoned them – from some darkness there emerged into the light with grotesque noise the like of which I had never heard, seven dogs. Had I not clearly seen that they were dogs, and that they were accompanied by their noise – though I was unable to see quite how they managed to produce it – I would have run off; but as it was, I stayed put.

At that time I understood almost nothing about the musicality exclusive to our species, it had managed to escape my burgeoning attention so far; there had been vague attempts to point me towards it, nothing more, and so much the more astonishing, yes, positively overwhelming was the impression made on me by these seven artistes. They didn't speak, they didn't sing, they tended to silence almost with a certain – forgive me – doggedness, but from empty space they contrived to conjure up music. All was music. The picking up and setting down of their feet, certain anglings of the head, their running and resting, the positions they took up towards one another, the recurring associations they entered with one another, with one, say, resting his forepaws on another's back, and then all seven performing this same action, so that the first bore the weight of all the others, or the way their bodies creeping low to the ground made tangled forms – never erring, not even the last of them who was still a little unsure of himself and didn't straight-away find the connection to those ahead of him, so to speak, in striking the tune, sometimes missed a cue, but that was only by comparison to the great certainty of the others, and even had his own relative uncertainty been far greater, a complete uncertainty, it would not have managed to spoil anything, while the others, the great masters, imperturbably kept the beat. But then I hardly saw them, I could hardly take them in. They had stepped forth. I had privately greeted them as dogs, though of course I was greatly confused by the sound that accom-panied them, but they had to be dogs, dogs like me and you. I looked at them through the eyes of habit, like dogs one might meet on the street. I felt like approaching them, for an exchange of greetings: they were very near to me, dogs a lot older than I was and not of my long-haired woolly kind, but nor were they that alien to me either in form and stature – they seemed somehow familiar, I knew many of their sort or similar sorts, but while I was still caught up in these reflections, the music gradually took over, veritably taking possession of me, pulling me away from these actual little dogs, quite against my will; in fact, while I was resisting it with all my might, howling like a dog in pain, I was permitted to occupy myself with nothing else but the music that came at me from all sides – from the heights, from the depths, from everywhere, taking the listener in its midst, flooding him, crushing him, even as he was annihilated, in such proximity that it felt remote, like barely audible fanfares in the distance. And then I was let go, because I was too exhausted, too destroyed, too weak to be able to hear; I was released, and I saw seven little dogs in a procession, doing their leaps. I felt like calling out to them, however disdainful they looked, to ask them for a lesson, ask them what they were doing here – I was a child after all, and thought I had a right to put my questions to all and sundry – but no sooner had I begun, no sooner had I felt the good familiar doggish connection with the seven than the music returned and drove me wild. I walked around in small circles, as though I myself was one of the musicians, whereas I was only their victim, flung myself this way and that, begging for mercy, and finally saved myself from its power only because it had forced me against a tangle of boards that seemed to have risen up in that place, without my having noticed it before, and now I was caught fast in it, it pressed my head down and, while the music was still thundering on in the open, made it possible for me to pause and catch my breath.

Truly, though, more than the artistry of the seven dogs – which was baffling to me, but also wholly impossible to account for, so totally beyond anything I knew – I was surprised at their courage in giving themselves over so wholly and openly to what they were producing, and at their strength to bear it so calmly, without it breaking their backs. I now began to see, on closer inspection from my little vantage point, that it wasn't so much calm as intense concentration with which they were working. Those apparently so securely stepping feet were in a continual fearful tremor; they looked at each other seemingly rigid with despair, and their tongues, which they made constant efforts to control, would then hang slackly from their muzzles. It couldn't be doubt of success that came over them; anyone who dared such a thing, or was capable of creating work of that order, surely couldn't be afraid. What was there for them to fear? Who compelled them to do what they were doing?

I was unable to restrain myself any longer, particularly once they seemed to me quite bafflingly in need of help, and so through all the noise I called out my questions loudly and peremptorily. They, though – baffling, baffling! – made no reply and ignored me, a breach of manners that under no circumstances is allowed the smallest or the greatest dog. So were they not dogs after all? But how could they not be dogs? Now, as I listened more closely, I heard the quiet words of encouragement they called to one another, pointing out difficulties ahead, warning each other of mistakes. I saw the least little dog, who was receiving the most calls, often squint in my direction, as though he wanted very badly to answer me, but was forcing himself not to, because he wasn't allowed. But why was it not allowed, how could the very thing that our laws unconditionally demand on this occasion not be permitted? My heart was outraged; I all but forgot the music. These dogs were in breach of the law. Great and magical artists they might be, but the law applied just as much to them, even as a child I understood that. And from then on I observed more and more. They really had good reason to be silent, assuming they were silent out of guilt. Because in the way they were carrying on – the music had blinded me to it so far – they had left all modesty behind: the wretches were doing the most ridiculous and obscene thing, they were walking upright on their hind legs. Faugh! They bared themselves, and exposed their nakedness to full view; they were proud of themselves and if they once obeyed a better impulse and dropped down onto their front legs, they positively shrank as though that had been a mistake, as though the whole of Nature was a mistake, and quickly lifted up their feet again. Their expression seemed to be asking forgiveness for briefly having interrupted their sinfulness.

Was the world out of kilter? Where was I? What had happened? At this point, for the sake of my own being, I could no longer hesitate. I freed myself from the embrace of the planks, leapt out with a single bound and made for the dogs – I, a little pupil, was called upon to be a teacher. I had to make them understand what they were doing, and keep them from further sin. 'Such old dogs, such old dogs!' I kept tutting away to myself. But no sooner was I free, and there were just two or three paces between me and them, there was the noise again, reasserting its sway over me. Perhaps in my zeal I could have overcome it this time, since I knew it better now, had it not been for the fact that in all its terrible but still resistible polyphony, a clear, stern, constant and unvarying tone was coming at me from ever so far away – perhaps it was the actual melody in the midst of the noise – that forced me to my knees. Oh, what beguiling music these dogs could make. I couldn't go on, I no longer wanted to lecture them; let them sprawl with their feet apart, commit sins and lead others to the sin of quiet spectating. I was such a small dog – who could demand something so difficult of me? I made myself even smaller than I was already, I whimpered, if the dogs had stopped and asked me for an opinion then, I might very well have agreed with them. In any case, it didn't go on for very much longer, and they disappeared with all their sound and light into the darkness from which they had sprung.

As I say, there was really nothing remarkable about the whole incident; in the course of a long life you will experience many things that, taken out of context and viewed through the eyes of a child, will be much more remarkable. And then, too, one can of course – as the expression goes – talk anything up. All that happened was that seven musicians had met to make music on a quiet morning, and a small dog had blundered upon them, an irritating spectator whom they tried, unfortunately in vain, to drive away by especially terrible or especially elevated music. If his questions were bothersome to them, were they, irked already by the mere presence of the stranger, to respond to this nuisance and add to it by providing answers? And even if the law instructs us to give answers to everyone, is such a tiny stray so-and-so even to be termed as anyone? Maybe they couldn't understand him; presumably he was lisping out his questions in a way that was hard to understand. Or perhaps they understood him perfectly well and mastered themselves to the extent of providing answers, but he, the little fellow, unused to music, couldn't tell the answers from the music. And as far as the business with the hind legs goes, maybe they really only walked like that on a few rare occasions. Yes, of course, it is a sin! But they were alone together – seven of them – a community of friends in the privacy of their own four walls, so to speak; quite alone, if you like, because to be among friends is not like being on public view, and then it takes more than the chance presence of a nosy little street-dog to make an occasion public; therefore, is it not the case instead that nothing really happened? Not quite, perhaps, but very nearly, and the lesson is that parents should keep their little ones from running around so much, and train them to remain silent and respect their elders.

If that is indeed so, then the case is settled. Though settled for grown-ups doesn't settle it for the little ones. I was running around, telling people, asking questions, making accusations, investigating and wanting to drag anyone at all off to the place where it had all happened, to show everyone where I had stood and where the seven had been and where and how they had danced and made music, and if anyone had been willing to go there with me, instead of shaking me off and laughing at me, then I would have been prepared to sacrifice my being without sin, and would have tried to get up on my hind legs, to make everything utterly clear. Well, people are hard on children, though in the end they tend to forgive them. It seems I have kept my childlike nature, even as I have grown into an old dog myself. And so I never stopped talking aloud about that incident, though I place less importance on it today, breaking it up into its component parts, trying it out on all and sundry without regard to the society in which I found myself, always thinking about the issue, bending the ears of others as my own were bent, only – and this was the major difference between us – I felt impelled to get to the bottom of it, so as to free my mind for the quiet satisfactions of day-to-day living. I have gone on applying myself, though with less childish means – the difference isn't as great as one might have expected – and yet even today I'm not much further along.

But it all began with that concert. I am not complaining, by the way, it's my inborn nature which, even if there had been no concert at all, would have found some other occasion to express itself. I only regretted the fact that it occurred so soon and took up such a lot of my childhood; the happy life of young dogs, that some are able to stretch out over many years, in my case was over in a matter of months. Well, never mind! There are more important things than childhood. And perhaps old age, worked for over the course of a hard life, will offer me more in the way of childish happiness than an actual child would have the strength to endure, though I now will.

It was then that I embarked on my investigations. I wasn't short of material: rather, the excess of it drove me to distraction in my dark hours. I began to study what keeps us dogs nourished. Now, of course that's not a straightforward question; it's what's been preoccupying us from time immemorial. It is the main object of our research; a vast body of observations and theories and opinions has been assembled on the topic, it has become a science whose dimensions exceed the comprehension not just of any given individual, but of the totality of all scholars, and can finally only be borne by nothing less than the entirety of dogdom, and even then only partially and not without complaint; because bits of long-held historic knowledge are continually crumbling away, demanding to be painfully replaced, not to mention the complexities and the scarcely possible demands of integrating the new learning.

So don't come to me with this objection. I know all that at least as well as the dog on the street; it doesn't occur to me to consider what I do as in any way scientific, I am full of healthy respect for science, but to add to it I lack the understanding and the application and the peace of mind and – not least, especially over the last few years – the appetite. I gulp my food down as and when I find it, but don't consider it worth my while to subject it to any methodical agricultural examination. In this respect I am content to abide by the accepted distillation of all wisdom, the little rule with which the mother sends her pup from her dugs out into the wide world: 'Wet everything as well as you can.' And doesn't that indeed say pretty much everything? What has science, launched by our forebears, substantially to add to that? Details, details, and how uncertain all that is, whereas this rule will endure as long as dogs are dogs. It concerns our principal food; admittedly, we have other, auxiliary sources, but in general, and if times aren't too hard, then we can live from this principal source that we can find on the ground, while what the ground needs from us is our water, which nourishes it, and it is at that price that it gives us our food, whose production – lest it be forgotten – can be accelerated by certain invocations, songs and ritual movements. But that really in my opinion is the sum total of everything that can usefully be said on the subject from this point of view. Here I am in full agreement with the great majority of dogdom, and I will have nothing to do with other views, which I consider to be heretical.

Truly, I am not concerned with special pleading or being proved right, I am happy to be in agreement with my fellows, and that is the case here. But my research leads me in another direction. I know from appearances that the earth, when sprinkled and worked according to all the rules of science, gives us nourishment in sufficient quantity and quality of such kinds, in such places, and at such times as accord with the principles partly or wholly established by science. I accept this, but my question remains: 'From where does the earth take this food?' A question many claim not to understand, and to which at best the answer comes: 'If you haven't got enough to eat, we'll give you some of ours.' Mark this answer. I know that sharing individually obtained food with the generality is not among the strong points of the canine community. Life is hard, the earth is mean; science, so rich in understanding, is less so in practical outcomes; whoever has food will keep it; nor is that to be termed selfishness – it's the opposite, it's the law of the dog, a unanimous popular decision, proceeding from the over-coming of selfishness, because those in possession are always in the minority. Hence the reply, 'If you haven't got enough to eat, we'll give you some of ours' is a joke, a tease, a *bon mot*. I have not forgotten that. But it had all the more significance for me because to me, going about the world with my questions, they left out the humorous aspect; I was still given nothing to eat – where would it have been obtained, in any case? And if someone just happened to have something, then of course, crazed with hunger as he was, any kind of compassionate regard was forgotten, but the offer was meant seriously and here and there I really did get the odd morsel, if I was quick enough to take possession of it. Why was it that others behaved so differently towards me? Favoured me, spared me? Because I was a feeble scrawny dog, badly fed, and too little concerned with nourishing myself? But the world is full of badly fed dogs and we like to snatch even the worst food from their chops, if we can – not out of greed, but on principle.

No, I received preferential treatment, not to the extent that I could prove it in detail, but that certainly was my firm impression. So was it my questions that gave pleasure, that were taken to be particularly thoughtful? No, they gave no pleasure and some even thought they were stupid. And yet it could only be my questions that gained me their attention. It was as though they would rather do the extraordinary thing and stuff my mouth with food – they didn't do it, but they wanted to – than attend to my questions. But then they would have done better to chase me away, and have done with my questions that way. But no, they didn't want to do that, they might not have wanted to hear my questions, but they didn't want to chase me away just because of them either. It was as if, no matter how much I was laughed at, treated as a silly little animal, pushed this way and that, it was actually the time I was treated with the greatest respect; never again did anything similar happen to me; I was able to go everywhere, nothing was kept from me; under the pretext of brusqueness I was actually given kid-gloved treatment. And it had to be all on account of my questions, my impatience, my desire to investigate. Did they want to lull me, lead me off the false path without violence – almost lovingly – from a path whose wrongness wasn't so self-evident that it might have permitted the use of violence; in any case, a certain respect and fear may have kept them from violence. At the time I sensed something of the sort; today I know it much better than those who did it to me then: they did indeed want to divert me from my path. They weren't successful; they achieved the opposite and my attentiveness was heightened. I even had the impression that it was I who wanted to lead the others, and to some extent my attempt was successful. It was only with help from the dog community that I began to understand what my own questions were about. If I asked, for example, where does the earth get the food from, did I care, as it might have appeared that I did, about the earth and its concerns? Not in the least, as I soon discovered, that was furthest from my thoughts – all I cared about were the dogs, nothing else. For what is there apart from dogs? To whom else can one appeal in an otherwise empty world? All science, the totality of all questions and all answers, lies with us dogs. If only one could make this science productive, bring it to the light of day. If only they didn't know so infinitely more than they admit, even to themselves. The most garrulous dog is laconic by comparison with those places that offer the best food. You slink around your fellow dog, you froth with avidity, you lash yourself with your tail, you ask, you beg, you howl, you bite and finally you achieve – well, you achieve what you would have achieved without any exertion: a kindly hearing, friendly touches, respectful snufflings, intimate embraces, my and thy howls commingle – everything tends to make you find oblivion in delight. But the one thing you wanted above all to achieve – confirmation of what you know – that remains denied to you; to that request, whether tacit or voiced, if you have taken wheedling and tempting as far as they will go, you will be treated at best to blank expressions, dull, veiled eyes, looks askance.

It's not so very different from the way it was back then, in my youth, when I called out to the musician dogs and they were silent. Now you might say: 'Here you are complaining about your fellow dogs and their silence on various crucial questions. You claim they know more than they're saying, more than they want to have said in their lives, and this silence, the reason and secret of which of course forms part of their silence, is poisoning your life, making it unendurable for you. You had to change it or quit it, maybe so, but aren't you a dog yourself, don't you have dog-knowledge? Well, tell us, not only in the form of a question, but as an answer. If you were to articulate it, who would be able to resist you? The great chorus of caninity would chime in with you, as if it had just been waiting for this moment. Then you would have truth, clarity, admission – as much as you wanted. The roof of the lowly life about which you have so many bad things to say will open, and we all, dog by dog, will rise through it into freedom and openness. And if the last should prove impossible, if it should all turn out to be worse than before, if the whole truth should be more unbearable than half the truth, if it should be confirmed that the silent ones are in the right because they are the sustainers of life, and should the slim hope we have now turn into utter helplessness, it will still have been worth the attempt, since you are unwilling to live as you are permitted to live. How can you hold their silence against others, and keep silent yourself?'

Easy answer: because I am a dog. Basically like the others, tight shut, offering resistance to my own questions, rigid with fear. Am I in fact, at least since I have become an adult, looking to dogdom for answers to my questions? Are my hopes so foolish? Do I see the foundations of our life, and sense their depth, watch the workers on the site, doing their grim work, and still expect that as far as my questions go, all that will be ended, torn down, abandoned? No, I really don't expect that any more. With my questions I am only chasing myself, driving myself on with the silence that is the only answer I get from all around me. How long do you think you can stand it that dogdom, which through your questions you are gradually bringing to consciousness, is silent and will always be silent? How long can you stand it: beyond all individual questions, that is the question of questions for my life; it's been put specifically to me, and troubles no one else. Unfortunately I can answer it more easily than the detailed, supplementary questions: I will presumably be able to stand it until my natural end – old age is placid and gets better and better at withstanding the restless questioning. I will probably die in silence, surrounded by silence, a peaceful death, and I am almost reconciled to it. An admirably strong heart and lungs not to be worn out ahead of time were given to us dogs almost out of malice, we resist all questions, even our own, being the barricade of silence that we are.

More and more often of late, thinking about my life, I seek out the decisive and fundamental mistake I have probably committed – and can't find it. And yet I must have committed it, because if I hadn't and had still not attained what I wanted to attain, in spite of the honest endeavours of a long life, then it would have been proof that what I wanted was impossible, and the consequence would be utter hopelessness. Behold thy life's work! First of all, there were my investigations on the question: from where does the earth take our food. A young pup, avid for life, I renounced all pleasures, avoided all entertainments, when tempted I buried my head between my legs, and set to work. This was no scientific task, neither in terms of erudition, or method, or purpose. They were my mistakes, yes, but I don't suppose they were decisive ones. I learned little, because I left my mother at an early age, roamed at large, and soon became accustomed to independence; premature independence is inimical to the systematic acquisition of knowledge. But I saw and heard many things. I talked to dogs of all sorts and degrees, and understood reasonably well what I was told; integrating single observations into the whole, that stood in to some extent for erudition, and besides, independence, though it may be a disadvantage where the acquisition of knowledge is concerned, yet for research it is a great advantage. It was all the more necessary in my case because I was unable to follow the proper scientific method, which would have been to use the work of predecessors and to seek out my scientific contemporaries. Instead, I was utterly self-reliant, I began at the very beginning, and with the awareness – so enchanting to the young, so profoundly dispiriting for the elderly – that whatever chance point I happened to reach would also define my whole endeavour. But was I really so alone with my investigations, all this time? Yes and no. It is impossible to think that the odd dog hasn't found himself – doesn't find himself today – in my situation. Things can't be that desperate for me. I am not a hair's breadth outside the doggish norm. Every dog has, as I do, the urge to question. And I, like all dogs, have the compulsion to be silent. All have the urge to ask questions. Could my questions otherwise have had the least effect, which I was fortunate enough to behold with delight, albeit greatly overstated delight? And the fact that I also have a compulsion to silence, that needs no particular support. Fundamentally, then, I am not so different from any other dog, and that is why basically everyone will recognize me and I them, despite the differences of opinion and taste that may exist between us. Only the proportion of the constituent elements varies; to me personally the difference is substantial, but in terms of the species as a whole it is negligible. How should the mixture of elements, either now or in the past, not have given rise to the likes of myself or even (if one wants to call the result unfortunate in my case), something still more unfortunate? Why, that would fly in the face of all experience. We dogs are busy in the most varied professions and callings, such professions as one would hardly credit, if it wasn't that one had the most reliable information about them.

I like to think at this point about air-dogs. The first time I heard of one such, I laughed and refused to be persuaded of their existence. What?! A minuscule dog, not much bigger than my head, even when fully mature, and this dog, utterly feeble of course – by appearances an artificial, immature, excessively coiffed thing, quite incapable of an honest to goodness leap – a dog like this was said to move largely through the air, and without any visible effort either, but to do so in a state of rest. No, to seek to convince me of such a thing was to take advantage of the earnest credulousness of a young dog, or so I thought. But then I heard tell, from a separate source, of a second air-dog. Was this some sort of conspiracy to make fun of me? This was when I encountered the musician dogs, and from that time forth, I thought everything was possible. I allowed no prejudice to set limits to my imagination, I pursued the most outrageous rumours, investigating them to the best of my ability; the most senseless things in this farraginous thing we call life seemed to be more plausible than any amount of sense, and in terms of my research, especially useful. These air-dogs were one example. I learned a lot about them, to this day I haven't actually seen one, but I became convinced of their existence long ago, and they occupy an important place in my overall scheme of things. As is usually the case, so here it is not the art that gives me pause. It's wonderful – who could deny it – that these dogs are able to float through the air: in my astonishment I am one with the rest of dogdom. But much more wonderful to me is the overall feeling of farrago, the silent unreasonableness of these beings. In general there is no cause given for it – they float through the air, and that's our lot; life goes on, here and there they talk of art and artists, and that's it. But why, oh kindly dogdom, why do these particular dogs float? What point is there in their calling? Why no word of explanation from the creatures themselves? Why do they float up there, letting their legs, which are our pride and joy, atrophy from being parted from the nourishing mother earth, not sowing, merely reaping, apparently even being nourished particularly well by providential dogdom.

I flatter myself that by my questions I may have stirred up these things. One begins to seek causes, to stammer together a kind of aetiology – yes, one begins, and of course will never get beyond the beginning. But it's something – a beginning. The truth may not appear – one won't get that far – but at least something of the deeply rooted nature of the lie. All the nonsensical aspects of life, most especially the most nonsensical ones, allow themselves to be justified. Not completely – that's the fiendish nature of what one is up against – but enough to guard against difficult questions. I'll take the air-dogs by way of example again. They are not arrogant, as one might at first have supposed; they are if anything perhaps especially needy of their fellow dogs. If you try and put yourself in their position, you will understand. Even if they can't do so openly – that would violate the rule of silence – they are obliged in one way or another to seek absolution for their way of life, or at least to distract from it, obscure it, which they do, so I am told, by their almost unbearable garrulousness. They are forever holding forth, whether about their philosophy, to which, since they have almost completely abandoned physical exertion, they are able to devote themselves, or about the observations they are able to make from their comparative altitude. And even though they don't shine in terms of their intellect, which is only too understandable given the frivolous nature of their lives, and their philosophy is as worthless as their observations so that they become almost useless to science, which fortunately doesn't depend on such miserable auxiliary sources, even so, when you ask what air-dogs are for, the answer you keep hearing is that they contribute an awful lot to science. 'True,' you reply, 'only it's a lot that is worthless and maddening.' The next answer is a shrug of the shoulders, a change of subject, a show of irritation or laughter, and in a while, the next time you ask, it is only to be told again that they contribute to science, and finally, should the question be put to you, you don't think about it too much and you make the very same reply. And maybe it's a good thing not to be too obdurate and to give in, maybe not conceding those air-dogs already extant have some purpose in their lives, which would be impossible, but at least to tolerate them. You can't ask for more than that, and then of course you do. You ask for tolerance to be extended to more and more air-dogs as they multiply. You don't exactly know where they come from. Do they procreate by the conventional method? Do they have the strength? After all there's not much more to them than a beautiful pelt, so what there is going to actually procreate? And if the improbable should happen, when would it take place? They are only ever seen in splendid isolation and if they condescend to run around at all, it's only for a little while, a few sashaying strides and always lost – it is claimed – in solitary thought, from which, even if they tried, they cannot break free. At least so they tell us. If these creatures don't manage to procreate, is it conceivable that dogs would come forward who freely renounce life on terra firma, in order to become air-dogs, and in exchange for a modicum of comfort and a certain technical prestige, choose that arid, pillowed life?

I say no. I think neither procreation nor voluntary renunciation is conceivable. But the facts prove to us that there are always new air-dogs around; from this we are driven to conclude that even if the hindrances are insuperable in our understanding, a breed of dogs once in existence and however peculiar will not be rendered extinct – or at least not easily, not without some aspect in each breed that will stick up for itself long and hard. And then, am I not compelled to think, if this holds true for such an eccentric, meaningless, visually freakish, unviable breed as the air-dog, will it not equally hold true for my own? And I am externally not at all out of the run of dogs that is very often met with, at least in these parts, in no way either conspicuous or contemptible; certainly in my youth and still to some degree into manhood, as long as I didn't neglect myself and took a modicum of exercise, I was a moderately attractive specimen, my front aspect especially came in for praise, my trim legs, the graceful carriage of my head, but also my grey-white-yellow fur, curling at the ends was much admired; but none of it stood out, the only remarkable thing about me is my nature, but even that, as I never tire of pointing out, is squarely rooted in the general canine character. Now, if the air-dog is not left celibate, and here and there in greater dogdom a willing individual is found, and they can produce heirs even *ex nihilo*, then why may I not be certain that I have not been abandoned? Of course my fellow dogs must have a particular destiny, and their existence will never visibly help me, not least because I will never acknowledge them. We are those who are oppressed by silence, who break it merely in order to breathe; the others seem to feel at ease in it, though that is only in appearance, as with the musical dogs, who were in harmony and apparent tranquillity, while in reality they were tremendously agitated. But the outward appearance is strong – one may seek to outwit it, but it mocks all our attempts.

So how do my fellow dogs help one another? What kind of attempts do they make to live in spite of everything? What do they look like? There are probably different answers. I tried with my attempts at questioning, while I was young. It might be an idea to stick to those who are given to asking questions themselves, and then, I would have some company. For a time I tried that too, in spite of myself, because the ones that most bother me are the ones from whom I want answers; the ones who keep butting in with questions I usually can't answer are merely repulsive to me. Anyway, who doesn't like to ask questions while he's still young? How am I to find the right ones among the many, many questioners? One question sounds much like another, it's a matter of the intention behind it, which is often concealed even from the questioner. Anyway, questioning is an idiosyncrasy among dogs; they ask their questions all at once, as though to conceal the traces of the real questioner. No, I won't find a confederate among the questioners, the young ones, any more than I do among the silent ones and the old ones, to whom I now belong. What's the point of questions anyway, I've failed with them; probably my fellow dogs are far cleverer than I am, and apply different and excellent methods of their own for coping with this life, methods, admittedly, that may be useful to them in appeasing or disguising who they are, may calm or lull or disguise what they are, but in general they will be just as ineffectual as mine because, look about me as I may, I see little sign of success in any quarter. I fear I will recognize a confederate by anything but success.

So where are they then? Yes, that's what lies at the heart of my complaint. Where are they? Everywhere and nowhere. It may be my neighbour, three steps away – we often call out to one another, he comes and sees me from time to time – I never visit him. So is he my twin soul? I don't know, I see nothing in him that I recognize, but it's possible. Possible, but hardly likely; if he's somewhere out of sight, in play and using all my imagination, I can indeed discern various suspiciously familiar qualities in him, but when I see him standing in front of me, I have to laugh at my fantasy. An old dog, a little shorter than I am (and I am barely average height), brown, short-haired, with a tired, drooping head, shuffling gait, and trailing his left hind leg, the consequence of some illness. I've not been on such close terms with anyone for a long time; I'm glad I can manage to tolerate him, and when he goes home I call out the friendliest things after him, not out of affection, but out of self-contempt, because as I watch him turn and go, I find him perfectly repulsive, the way he slinks off with that dragging foot of his and his hindquarters so dismally low to the ground. Sometimes I have the feeling I'm humiliating myself when I think of him as an associate at all. In our conversations he certainly doesn't indicate any sort of association: he is clever, and by our standards here, fairly cultured, and I'm sure there's much I could learn from him, but is it really cleverness and culture I'm looking for? We mostly talk about parochial things and I am regularly astonished – sensitized as I am in this respect by my solitariness – how much mind is required even for an ordinary dog, even in normal, not unduly adverse circumstances, to preserve himself from the standard perils of life. Science gives us rules, but understanding them only from a distance and in rough outline is not easy, and if one has understood them, then the difficult part begins, which is how they apply to local conditions. Hardly anyone can help you with that, almost every hour poses new problems, and every new patch of ground has special difficulties; no one can claim to be well-set for the long run, or that his life takes care of itself, not even I, whose requirements seem to dwindle from one day to the next. And all this effort – to what end? Only to bury yourself so deeply in silence that no one will ever be able to pull you out of it.

We like to celebrate the progress of dogdom; though probably what we mean is the progress of science. Indeed, science makes great strides, it is unstoppable; it even seems to accelerate, move ever more quickly, but what is worth celebrating about that? It's as if someone were to make a great fuss of becoming older with the passing years and approaching death ever more rapidly. I call that a natural process, and not even an attractive one at that, and I find nothing worth celebrating in it. All I see is decline, by which I don't mean that previous generations were superior – no, they were just younger, their memory was not so burdened as ours today, it was easier to get them to speak, and even if no one succeeded in doing it, the sense of possibility was greater, and it is this greater potential that so rouses us as we listen to those old, really rather unsophisticated stories. Every now and again we hear a promising word, and it's almost enough to get us to leap up, if it wasn't that we felt the burden of the centuries weighing us down. No, whatever I have against my own time, previous generations were no better, and in some respects they were much feebler and much worse. Miracles weren't performed in the streets then to be apprehended by all and sundry, but the dogs were somehow – I can think of no other way of saying this – not as doggish as they are today, dogdom was more loosely associated, the true word could have played a role, to change or revise the structure, at anyone's will, even turning it into its opposite, and the word at least felt close at hand, it was on the tip of the tongue, anyone could learn it. Today, where has it got to, today one could reach into the bowels of language and not find it! Our generation may be lost, but it is more innocent than its predecessors. I can understand our hesitation; in fact it's no longer just hesitation, it's the forgetting of a dream dreamed and forgotten for the first time a thousand nights ago. Who would hold it against us that we have forgotten it for the thousandth time?

But I can understand the hesitation of our forefathers too. We probably wouldn't have behaved any differently: I almost feel like saying, good for us, that it wasn't us who had to shoulder the guilt; rather that, in a world already darkened by others, we had to hasten towards death in an almost guilt-free silence. When our forefathers lost their way, they probably wouldn't have thought of an unending wilderness; they could probably still see the crossroads and it would have been easy enough to return there at any time, so only because they wanted to enjoy their dog's lives a little longer – it wasn't really a dog's life, and if it already struck them as intoxicatingly lovely, imagine what it would be like later, at least a little later – they wandered on. They didn't know what we can now sense from our contemplation of history, that the soul changes faster than life does, and that when their dog's life began to please them, they must already have had ancient souls, and they weren't as close to the starting point as maybe they thought, or as their eye, delighting in all those doggish joys, tried to convince them was the case. Who today can still speak of youth in any meaning-ful way? They were the true young dogs, but unfortunately their only ambition was to become old dogs, something they couldn't fail at, as every subsequent generation proves, and ours, the latest, proves best of all.

All these were things that of course I didn't speak of to my neighbour, but I often think of them when sitting with him, that typical old dog, or bury my muzzle in his fur, which already has something of the smell of a carcass. It would be pointless to talk about those things, with him or anyone else. I know what course the conversation would follow. He would offer a few little objections here and there, but in the end he would agree with me – agreement is our best defence – and the issue would be laid to rest. Why even bother digging it up in the first place? And yet, in spite of everything, there is perhaps a deeper accord with my neighbour that goes beyond mere words. I won't stop insisting on it, even though I have no evidence for it, and am perhaps subject simply to a very basic delusion, because he's the only party I've been in communication with for a long time, and so I am obliged to stick to him. 'Are you perhaps my comrade after all? In your own way? And you're ashamed because it's all gone wrong? See, I feel exactly the same way. When I'm alone, I cry about it; come, if there are two of us, it'll be sweeter.' That's what I think sometimes and fix his eye. He doesn't lower his glance, but there's nothing to be heard from him either; he looks at me expressionlessly, and wonders why I have allowed a break in our conversation, and don't say anything. But perhaps that look is his way of asking, and I disappoint him, just as he disappoints me. In my youth, if no other questions had seemed more important to me and I had had enough of myself, then I might have asked him out loud, might have got his quiet agreement in response, less than today, when he's silent. But isn't everyone silent? What keeps me from believing that they're all my comrades, that I didn't just find the occasional fellow researcher, sunk and forgotten along with his insignificant results, inaccessible beyond the darkness of the times, or the hustle of the present; but instead that I have had comrades in everyone always, all of them, in keeping with their nature, trying hard, all without success, all taciturn or gabby, as is inevitable. But then I would never have had to keep myself separate, I could have remained among the others, wouldn't have had to barge my way out like an ill-bred child through lines of grown-ups, who all wanted to go as much as I did, and whose sense is all that confuses me, that tells them that no one will get out, and that all attempts to push are foolish.

Such thoughts are undoubtedly influenced by my neighbour; he confuses me, he makes me melancholy; and yet he's happy enough by himself, at least when I hear him on his patch, calling out and singing in that irritating way of his. It would be good to dispense with this last element of society, not to pursue vague dreams of the sort that any dealings with dogs are bound to produce, no matter how tough you think you've become, and to use the little bit of time remaining to me exclusively for my investigations. The next time he comes calling, I will hide away and pretend to be asleep, and I will do that until he finally gives up altogether.

Also a measure of disorganization has crept into my research. I am falling behind, I am getting tired, I just trot along mechanically, where once I would leap ahead enraptured. I'm thinking back to the time when I first began to investigate the question 'Where does the earth take our nourishment from?' Then, admittedly, I lived amongst the crowd, I forced my way in where they were at their densest, I wanted everyone to be a witness to my work, their observations were even more important to me than my work, since I was still in expectation of some sort of general effect. That of course gave me huge encouragement, which as a solitary dog I no longer get. At that time, though, I was so strong that I did something unheard of, something that flies in the face of all our princples, and that any eyewitness from the time will recall as extraordinary. I found in one aspect of the science, which generally favours extreme specialization, a curious simplification. It teaches us that it is principally the earth that produces our food, and, having stated that, goes on to list the methods by which the various foods can be produced in their best condition and their greatest abundance. Now it's true of course, food does come from the ground, there is no doubting that, but it's really not so simple as in that bald statement, to the extent that it excludes all further research. Take the type of primitive incident that occurs every day. If we were wholly idle (as I in fact already almost am) and after perfunctorily tending the soil we rolled ourselves up and waited for what was coming, then we would indeed find our food on the ground – assuming, that is, that there was any food forthcoming at all. But this is hardly the rule. Whoever has managed to retain a modicum of open-mindedness vis-à-vis the science – and there are not many, as the circles that science likes to trace are ever-expanding – will easily see, even in the absence of specific observations, that the greater part of the nourishment on the ground will have come from above; sometimes, depending on our dexterity and the degree of our hunger, we even manage to intercept most of it before it touches the ground at all. Now, I'm not saying anything against the science; of course it's the earth that produces this nourishment, whether it summons it up from itself or calls it down from above hardly matters, and the science that has established that working the ground is necessary perhaps doesn't need to get itself involved in any more detail than that; after all, as we like to say: 'If you've got your munchies in your mouth, your problems are over for the time being.' But it seems to me that at least in a veiled way, science is partly concerned with these things, seeing that it does acknowledge there are two principal methods of sourcing food, namely working the soil and then the subtly complementary activities of speech, dance and song. While this may not be a complete dichotomy, it does seem to bear out my distinction. In my opinion, tilling the ground works to secure both types of nourishment and is always indispensable; speech, dance and song are less concerned with ground provisioning in the strict sense, and more with the drawing down of sustenance from above. In adopting this view, I am supported by tradition. Here the populace corrects science without apparently knowing it, and without science daring to oppose it. If, as science likes to claim, those ceremonies are exclusively concerned with serving the soil, say by giving it strength, then to be logical they would have to be performed on the ground, and everything would have to be whispered, chanted and danced in the direction of the ground. So far as I know, that's what science would have us do anyway. But here's the thing: the popular ceremonies are directed at the air. It's not a violation of science, science doesn't seek to stamp it out, it leaves the ploughman his discretion; in its teachings it is focused entirely on the soil, and if the ploughman performs these teachings on the ground, then it is satisfied, but its thinking, to my mind, should really be more sophisticated. And I, who was never deeply inducted into science, cannot for the life of me imagine how learned men can tolerate our people, passionate as they are, calling out the magic words into the

air, wailing our old folk lamentations at the air, and performing leaping dances as if quite forgetting the ground,
they wanted to hang in the air forever. My starting point
was to stress these contradictions. Each time that,
according to the principles of science, harvest time drew
near, I confined my attentions to the soil; I scraped it in
my dancing, I twisted my head to be as close to it as
I could; later I dug a furrow for my muzzle and sang and
declaimed in such a way that only the ground might hear
it and no one else above me or beside me.

The results of my research were inconclusive: sometimes I was given no food and was on the point of
jubilation about my discovery, but then the food pre-
sented itself, as though initially perplexed by the
eccentricity of my original performance. And now, seeing its advantages, and happy to dispense with my shouts
and leaps, often the food came more abundantly than
before, though there were other times when none was
forthcoming at all. With an industry unknown previously
in young dogs, I kept exact records of all my experiments,
and from time to time thought I had found a sign that
would take me further, but then it was lost in the sand.
Impossible to deny, too, that my lack of scientific back-
ground was a handicap. How could I prove for instance
that the unforthcomingness of food was not brought on
by some fault with my experiment – unscientific tilling

of the ground, for instance – and if that was the case, then all my results were void. There was a perfectly precise experiment I could have conducted, that is, if I had succeeded without preparing the ground at all and then purely through a vertically directed ceremony in getting the lowering of the food, while by groundwork alone the food had failed to appear. I attempted something of the kind, but without real conviction and not under laboratory conditions, because I remain unshakeably convinced that a certain measure of preparing the ground is essential; and even if those heretics who don't believe it were right, it still couldn't be proved, since the sprinkling of the ground takes place under pressure and up to a point is not wholly voluntary. I had more success with a different, rather unusual experiment that attracted a certain amount of attention. In a variant of the usual interception of food in mid-air, I decided not to allow the food to fall to the ground, but not to intercept it either. To that end, I would perform a little leap in the air that was calculatedly inept; usually what happened was that it fell dully to the ground, and I would hurl myself upon it in a fury, not just of hunger but of disappointment. But in a few cases, something else happened, something actually rather miraculous: the food would not drop, but would follow me in the air – the food would follow the hungry individual. This didn't take place in any sustained way – just for brief spells – and then it would fall after all, or disappear altogether or – this was the usual outcome – my greed would bring a premature end to the experiment and I wolfed down whatever it was.

Still, I was happy at the time, there was a buzz around me, others were unsettled by me and began to take an interest, I found my acquaintances more open to my questions, in their eyes I saw the appeal for help; and even if it was nothing more than the reflection of my own look, I wanted nothing more, I was content. Until I learned – and others learned with me – that this experiment had been written up in science long ago, in a far grander version than mine, though it hadn't been performed for a long time because of the degree of self-control it calls for, and also on account of its alleged scientific insignificance. It proved, so they said, only what was already known, namely that the ground does not collect nourishment in a direct vertical line, but at an angle, or even in a spiral.

So there I was, but I wasn't at all discouraged, I was much too young for that; on the contrary, I felt emboldened to attempt what was perhaps the greatest achievement of my life. I didn't believe that my experiment was ultimately discredited, but this wasn't a question of belief, but of proof, and I wanted to acquire it, and thus place my originally somewhat eccentric experiment under the harsh light and focus of science. I wanted to prove that when I shrank back from the nourishment, it wasn't the ground that drew it down at an angle, but myself drawing it on to me. I wasn't able to expand the experiment; to see the munchies in front of me and to go on experimenting scientifically is more than any dog can stand in the long run. But I purposed something else. I wanted to go on a fast for as long as I could bear it, while avoiding all sight of food and all temptation. If I withdrew in such a fashion, remained lying there with eyes closed day and night, attempted neither the picking up nor the intercepting of food, and as I didn't dare claim but privately hoped, without any of the usual measures save the inevitable uncontrolled irrigation of the soil and quiet recital of speech and song (I would renounce the function of dance so as not to weaken myself), the food would descend of its own accord and, without bothering with the ground, would crave entry by knocking against my teeth – if this were to happen, then I wouldn't have overturned the science, because science is sufficiently elastic for exceptions and isolated cases, but what would the people say, who happily possess less in the way of elasticity? After all, this wouldn't be an exception of the sort that is handed down in stories – someone, say, with a physical malady or mental impairment refusing to work for their food, to look for it, or to consume it, upon which dogdom would assemble and recite formulas of invocation and secure a movement of the food from its usual path directly into the mouth of the afflicted party. I was in the pink, my appetite was so healthy that for days I could think of nothing else; I submitted, believe it or not, voluntarily to fasting, I was myself fully responsible for the downward course of the nourishment, I needed no help from dogdom, and even explicitly forbade it.

I sought out an appropriate place in a remote shrubbery where I would hear no talk of food, no smacking of lips or cracking of bones, filled my belly one last time, and then lay down. It was my idea to spend all the time if possible with my eyes closed; so long as no food came, it should be night as far as I was concerned, and it would go on for days and weeks. The great difficulty was that I should not sleep either, or at least as little as possible, because I had not only to be summoning down the food to me, but also I had to be on guard lest I sleep through its coming; on the other hand, of course sleep was most welcome, because I would be able to go on fasting for much longer asleep than awake. With these thoughts, I decided to divide my time very carefully and sleep a lot, but only in very short spells. I managed this by propping my head on a thin branch that would quickly bend and thereby wake me. So there I lay, asleep or awake, dream ing or silently singing to myself. To begin with, time passed wholly uneventfully, perhaps it had not been observed, wherever food was distributed, that I was absent, opposing the usual run of things, and so all was quiet. I was a little disturbed in my endeavour by the fear that the dogs would miss me, find me and undertake some action against me. A second fear was lest, in response to a mere sprinkling, the ground, even though by the light of science it was infertile ground, would provide some so-called inadvertent nourishment, and its smile could beguile me. But for the moment nothing like that happened, and I was able to go on starving myself. My fears aside, I was quite calm to begin with, in a way I can't remember having been before. Even though I was working against science, I felt a great contentment – almost the proverbial calm of the scientific worker. In my dreams I obtained science's indulgence; I felt assured that it also had room for my inquiries, it sounded very soothing in my ears that, however successful my research ended up being (and especially then), I would not be lost to the ordinary life of dogs; science cast a kindly eye on me, it promised it would get to work on the interpretation of my findings, and that promise to me was fulfilment itself; I would, even as I felt expelled in my innermost being, and charged the walls of my tribe like a wild thing, I would be received with honours, the longed-for warmth of assembled dogsbodies would flow around me, I would be carried swaying, shoulder high by my people. Hunger can have a powerful effect on those unaccustomed to it. My achievement seemed to me such that out of self-pity I began to cry in my shrubbery, which didn't quite make sense since, if I was expecting the reward I'd earned, why cry? Out of sheer contentment. I never liked to cry. Whenever I felt satisfaction, which was rarely enough, I cried. At least it was soon over. The pretty pictures faded gradually as my hunger grew, and it didn't take long until fantasies and emotion had been purged and I was completely alone with the burning sensation in my intestines. 'That's what hunger feels like,' I said to myself endlessly, as though to persuade myself that hunger and I were still two separate beings, and I could shake it off like a tedious lover, but in reality we were a very painful entity, and when I said to myself, 'That's what hunger feels like', then it was really hunger that was speaking and thus making fun of me. An awful, awful time! I still shudder to remember it, not just on account of the suffering I endured, but because I didn't see it through to the end, because I will have to go through this hunger again if I am to achieve anything, because starvation is to me still the ultimate and most powerful tool in my investigations. The way leads through starvation; the highest is only attainable through the most extreme privation, and for us this privation is voluntary fasting.

So when I think back to those times – and I love to brood over them – I think too about the times that loom ahead. It seems you have to almost let your life pass by before you recover from such an experiment; my entire manhood separates me from that period of starvation, and I still haven't recovered. When next I embark on a period of starvation, I may have more resolve, as a result of my years and my superior understanding of the need for such an experiment, but my forces are still depleted from last time, I can feel myself sapped already by the prospect of the familiar terrors. My weaker appetite won't help me; at most it will devalue my experiment and probably force me to starve for longer than I would have had to then. I think I am clear about these and other assumptions, it's not that the long time in between has been without trial runs – often enough I have clamped my teeth round hunger, but I wasn't strong enough for the ultimate test – and the uninhibited get-up-and-go of youth is of course gone now. It faded while I was fasting that first time.

Some considerations tormented me. I saw the menacing spectres of our forefathers. Though I don't say so openly, I blame them for everything: they brought us the dog's life, and I could easily reply to their threats with

counter-threats of my own; but I bow to their knowledge, it came from sources that are no longer known to
us, which is why, however much I am opposed to them,
I would never disregard their laws, but just beetle towards
the little chinks in them for which I have a keen percep-
tion. Where hunger is concerned, I appeal to a famous
conversation in the course of which one of our sages
pronounced the intention of outlawing starvation, from
which another tried to dissuade him with the question:
'Who would ever think of starving themselves?' and the
former allowed himself to be persuaded and dropped the
idea of the ban. Now the question comes around again:
'Isn't starving yourself actually forbidden?' The great
majority of commentators deny it, they see fasting as
lawful, they take the part of the second wise man and
are therefore not afraid of bad consequences flowing
from their misleading comment. I had taken care to
ascertain the facts before embarking on my programme.
But now that I was writhing with hunger, and in my
mental confusion kept having recourse to my hind legs,
desperately licking, gnawing, sucking them all the way
up to my bottom, the general interpretation of that conversation struck me as completely false. I cursed the
commentators' science, I cursed myself for having
allowed myself to be misled by them; the conversation
contained, as any child would see – given that it was a

starving child – more than one ban on fasting; the first wise man wanted to forbid it, and whatever one wise man wants to do is already done, so hunger was already outlawed; and the second wise man not only agreed with him but even took hunger to be impossible, in effect balancing a second embargo on top of the first, this embargo deriving from the canine character itself; the first one understood this and therefore withheld the explicit embargo, that is, after discussion, he urged dogs to be prudent and simply to forswear starvation. In effect, it was a triple ban instead of the usual single one, and I had violated it.

Now I could at least have heeded it belatedly and stopped starving myself, but running right through the pain was a kind of temptation, and I followed its trail, as if lusting after an unknown scent. I couldn't stop, perhaps I was already too weak to get up and return to inhabited areas. I tossed and turned on my forest floor, sleeping was beyond me, I heard sounds everywhere; the world that had been asleep through my previous life seemed to have been brought to life by my hunger, I had the notion that I would never eat again, because then I would have to silence the whole world, and that was beyond me; admittedly the very loudest noise of all was in my stomach; I often pressed my ear against it and must have looked appalled because I could hardly believe what I was hearing. And as things were really getting bad, my senses became disorientated as well, and I thought of crazy ways of saving myself: I started smelling foods, exquisite things I hadn't eaten for ages, the joys of my infancy, yes, I could smell the teats of my mother. I forgot my resolve to resist smells, or rather I didn't; with determination, as though it were a resolution I'd set myself, I dragged myself around every which way, never more than one or two paces, and sniffed, as though I were seeking out foods so as to guard myself against them. The fact that I didn't find any didn't disappoint me, the food must be there, only it was always a few paces too far away for me, and my legs buckled before I could reach it. Simultaneously I knew that there was nothing there at all, that I was just carrying out these little movements for fear of the moment I would irrevocably break down somewhere and would never be able to leave. My last hopes disappeared, the last temptations: I would die miserably here, what was the point of my investigations, childish experiments from a childishly happy time; what was serious was here and now, here was where investigation could have proved its worth, but where was it? Here was a dog snapping at nothing, hurriedly and convulsively irrigating the soil over and over, though his memory was incapable of summoning a single line from the whole array of magical sayings, not even the one with which newborns take shelter under their mother.

I felt as though I wasn't just separated by a few yards from my brothers, but was infinitely far from all of them, and as though it wasn't hunger that was killing me so much as my sense of abandonment. It was perfectly clear that no one was bothering about me, no one under the ground, no one over the ground, no one in the heights; I was dying from indifference, the indifference was saying: he is dying, and so it would be. And didn't I agree? Wasn't I saying the same thing? Had I not in fact wanted this abandonment? Yes, you dogs, but not to end here like this, to reach across to the truth from out of this world of lies, where there is no one from whom you can learn the truth, not even me, a born citizen liar. Perhaps the truth wasn't all that far off, but it was too far for me, who was failing and would die. Perhaps it wasn't too far, and then I wasn't as abandoned as I thought either – not by the others, only by myself, failing and dying here.

But the truth is you don't die as quickly as an anxious dog believes. I merely lost consciousness, and when I came round and opened my eyes, there was an unfamiliar dog standing in front of me. I had no feeling of hunger, I felt very strong, in my joints there was a quivering, even though I made no attempt to test it by getting up. I didn't seem to see any more than I did at other times, and yet a fine but hardly outstanding dog was standing in front of me. I saw that – nothing else – and yet I thought I saw more of him than I would ordinarily. There was blood underneath me – my first thought was that it was food, but I noticed soon enough that it was blood that I had vomited. I turned away from it, and towards the strange dog. He was lean, long-legged, tan, here and there with flecks of white, and he had a fine, strong, questing look. 'What are you doing here?' he said. 'You must leave.' 'I can't leave now,' I said, without further explanation, because how could I have told him everything, and anyway he seemed to be in a hurry. 'Please, leave,' he said, restlessly picking up his feet in turn. 'Let me be,' I said. 'Go away and forget about me; just like the others have forgotten about me.' 'Please, for your own sake,' he said. 'You can ask me for anyone's sake you want,' I said, 'the fact is I can't leave, even if I wanted to.' 'That's not the issue,' he said, smiling. 'You can go. It's because you seem to be weak that I'm begging you to leave in your own time. If you hesitate, you'll only have to run later on.' 'Let that be my concern,' I said. 'It's mine too,' he said, grieved by my stubbornness, and it was obvious he would have preferred me to stay for the moment, and use the opportunity to approach me in love. At any other time, I would have submitted to such a handsome beast gladly, but just then,

I don't know why, I felt aghast at the idea, 'Go away,'
I screamed, all the more loudly as I had no other way of
defending myself. 'All right, I am going,' he said, slowly
stepping back. 'You're strange. Don't you like me then?'
'I will like you once you leave me alone,' I said, but I
wasn't as sure of myself as I wanted to sound. There was
something about him that I could hear or see with my
senses sharpened by hunger; it was just beginning, it was
growing, it was coming nearer, and already I knew: this
dog has the power to drive you away even if you can't
yet imagine how you will ever get to your feet. And
I looked at him, shaking his head gently at my coarse
reply, with ever greater desire. 'Who are you?' I asked.
'I'm a hunter,' he said. 'And why don't you want to leave
me here?' 'You're in the way,' he said. 'I can't hunt with
you here.' 'Try,' I said, 'perhaps you will be able to.' 'No,'
he said, 'I'm sorry, but you need to go.' 'Forget about
hunting for the day!' I asked him. 'No,' he said, 'I've got
to.' 'I've got to leave, and you've got to hunt,' I said. 'Lots
of 'gots' there. Do you understand why?' 'No,' he said,
'but there's nothing to understand either, these are all
perfectly reasonable, natural things.' 'Not at all,' I said,
'you're sorry to have to chase me away, and still you do
it.' 'That's true,' he said. 'That's true,' I mimicked crossly,
'what kind of answer is that? What would be easier for
you: not to hunt or not to drive me away?' 'Not to hunt,'

53

he said without any hesitation. 'Well then,' I said, 'you're contradicting yourself.' 'Where's the contradiction?' he asked. 'You dear little dog, don't you understand that I have to? Don't you understand perfectly natural things?' I didn't say anything because I noticed – and a kind of new life surged through me, a life that was sparked by a sense of dread – noticed from certain elusive details that maybe no one but me could have noticed, that this dog was opening his chest to make ready to sing. 'You're about to sing,' I said. 'Yes,' he said seriously, 'I'm going to sing – soon, but not yet.' 'You're already beginning,' I said. 'No,' he said, 'not yet. But prepare yourself.' 'Deny it all you want, I can hear it,' I said, trembling. He made no reply. And I thought I could tell what no dog before me had ever noticed – at least in our traditions there are no hints of it – and in endless panic and shame I hurriedly lowered my face to the puddle of blood in front of me. I thought I could tell that the dog was already singing without knowing it, yes, and more, that the melody, separate from him, was floating through the air following its own laws, through him and past him, as though it wasn't anything to do with him, and was only aiming for me. Today of course I will deny all such perceptions and merely ascribe them to my over-stimulated condition, but even if it was an illusion, it does have something magnificent about it, as the only apparent reality I managed to salvage from that period of starvation, and shows how far we can travel if we are completely beside ourselves, as I was then.

And I really was beside myself then. Under normal circumstances, I would have been seriously ill and unable to move, but I couldn't withstand the melody the dog would soon take up as his. It grew ever stronger; its welling seemed to know no bounds, already it was almost shattering my hearing. But the worst thing was that it seemed to exist only on my account, the voice before whose loftiness the forest hushed, was just for me; and who was I to dare to stay here sprawled out in front of it in blood and filth. Shaking, I got to my feet and looked down the length of my body; 'that body can't walk', I managed to think to myself, but already chased by the melody, I was flying along in exquisite bounds. I said nothing of this to my friends; right after my arrival I would probably have blabbed, but I was too weak, and later on it simply struck me that such things could not be communicated. Hints that I couldn't force myself to suppress were lost without trace in our conversations. Physically, I was restored in a matter of hours, though my spirit still bears the scars today.

I expanded the scope of my investigations to include canine music. Science had not been idle in this field either; the study of music, if I am correctly informed, is perhaps even more extensive than that of food and certainly more solidly based. This can be accounted for because the terrain can be worked over more dispassionately; it tends to be a matter of observation and systematization, whereas in that other field there are practical consequences to be weighed up as well. Connected to this is the fact that respect for musical science is greater than that for nutritional science, though the first can never be as deeply rooted in our people. Also my attitude towards musical science was more agnostic than any other – until I heard the voice in the forest. My experience with the canine musicians had already pointed me the way, but I was still too young at the time, nor is it easy to get to grips with that science; it is reckoned to be particularly arcane, and inaccessible. Also, while the music had been the most arresting aspect of those dogs, what seemed more important to me then was the discretion of their being, their terrible music was like nothing I had ever known, making it easier for me to set it aside, whereas their nature was what I encountered in dogs everywhere. To penetrate the true nature of dogs, the study of nutrition seemed to promise the most direct route. Perhaps I was wrong to think so. The contiguity of the two sciences had already caught my attention. It's the lesson of the song that brings down nourishment. Again, it is much to my regret that I never made a serious study of musical science; I can't even count myself among those semi-educated individuals who attract the most contempt from experts. I need to keep this in mind always. Given an elementary test by an expert, I would fare badly indeed – and unfortunately I have proof of this. This has its roots, in addition to my biographical circumstances mentioned already, in my lack of scientific ability, poor capacity for abstract thought, worse memory, and above all my inability to keep a scientific goal always before me. I admit all this to myself quite openly, even with a certain relish. Because the deeper ground for my scientific inability seems to me to be an instinct, and not a bad instinct at that. Were I to brag, I could say that it was this instinct that has destroyed my abilities as a scientist, because wouldn't it be odd after all, if I – who in the ordinary things of daily living, which are certainly not the simplest, demonstrate a tolerable comprehension, if not of science, then at least of scientists, as witness my results – if I should have been unable from the very beginning to raise my paw to the lowest rung of science. This was the instinct that – perhaps out of regard for science, but a different sort of science from that practised today, an ultimate science – has led me to esteem freedom more highly than anything else. Freedom! Freedom as it is on offer to us today is a wretched weed. But it's freedom of a kind, something to possess.